Hanako and Ken are staying with their grandmother and grandfather. Granny and Granddad live in a small town by the sea. In the summer, the town has lots of visitors and lots of things going on. Hanako and Ken go swimming in the sea every day.

I0824949

One day, Hanako and Ken see some trucks and trailers arrive and park on the common. The next day they see that a big tent has been put up, with a banner saying, “The Light-as-Air Circus.”

Several trailers are arranged in a circle around the big tent, and there is a smaller tent with a notice saying, “tickets.”

A girl with long red and blue hair is hula-hooping next to the ticket tent. She stops, smiles, and says, "Hi, I'm Sam. Are you here to get tickets?"
Hanako and Ken nod and pay for their tickets.
"See you tomorrow! I hope you all enjoy the show," Sam calls after them.

The next evening, Hanako, Ken, and their grandparents wait for the circus to begin. A man runs into the ring.
"Good evening!" he shouts, and everybody cheers.
"I am Gentleman George, your ringmaster, and that means I am in charge of the show."

Everyone claps.
"We hope to make you say 'ooh!' We hope to make you say 'ah!'" he shouts.

"Our first act..." he continues, but then there is a loud noise behind him. BANG! BANG! A car, driven by two clowns, comes into the ring. Smoke is billowing from the car. The clowns jump out and start spraying foam around.

"What are you..?" splutters Gentleman George before the clowns spray foam all over his head, bundle him into the car and drive him away.

Two more clowns race in and run around the edge of the ring before crashing into each other and landing on the floor. They stand up, and one says, “Excellent! Now that we have got rid of him, we are in charge! Hooray!”

The other clown turns to face everyone and says, “He thinks our jokes are terrible and nobody wants to listen to them, but you want to hear them, don’t you?”

"How do you build a flea circus?" says the first clown.
"You start from scratch!" replies the other clown.
Everybody groans and claps.

Then a man's head pops out from behind the curtain. "Where is George?" the man says. The clowns say, "Shhhhh!" as the children all shout and point at them. "We don't know where he is, but it's not a problem. We'll introduce you!" the clowns say. "Our first act, all the way from Moscow, is the Family Borlov!"

Eight acrobats tumble into the ring. They jump and turn, balance on their hands, and balance on each other. At the end of the act there is a drum roll. The acrobats start to climb up and stand on each other's shoulders to make a very tall and wobbly tower.

Then the smallest acrobat runs and jumps, and twists in the air, landing on top of the tower. Everyone claps and cheers. Then the acrobats tumble down and run out of the ring.

Next, the clowns set up a tightrope. One starts walking across the rope, falls off, rolls, and jumps up. "What does a tightrope walker have for breakfast?" he shouts.
"I don't know, what *does* a tightrope walker have for breakfast?" says the other clown.
"A balanced diet!" shouts the first clown.
Everyone groans again.

Then, the real tightrope walker, Purple Empress, enters. She holds her arms out to show her costume. It looks like giant butterfly wings. Everyone claps. She climbs up and starts to walk across the tightrope.

Suddenly, a man dressed as a butterfly collector runs in carrying a huge net. He swooshes the net several times, trying to catch the Purple Empress. Each time, she jumps, the net misses her, and she lands back on the tightrope. Then the crowd cheers as the clowns chase the man away.

“Next, we have the Bee Careful Jugglers,” announces one of the clowns.
“You know, I juggled bricks once,” shouts one of the other clowns. “I never knew why juggling bricks was a such bad idea until one hit me!”
The jugglers run in, juggling bean bags that look like bees. They juggle more and more bean bags until it looks like the air is full of bees.

A clown backs out from behind the curtain. "Look out!" scream the children. He takes another step back... and BUMP! The juggler and the clown collapse, and the bean bags fly all over the place. The jugglers look angry. "You are spoiling our act! Where is Gentleman George?" they shout. "He is supposed to be in charge here."

The clowns all shrug and try to look innocent. Then one turns, smiles and shouts, "Why don't elephants ride bikes?"
"We don't know!" everybody shouts.
"Because they don't have thumbs to ring the bell!"
All the clowns giggle.

"Now, please put your hands together for the Wibbly Wobbly Wheelers!" they shout.
A unicyclist rides in, followed by another, and then two more. Each unicyclist gets taller and taller.

When the Wibbly Wobbly Wheelers have finished, the clowns run back out into the ring again. "We *love* being in charge," they shout. "You all like us being in charge, don't you?"
Everybody claps.

"Now for our final act: The Black Widow Spider," announces one of the clowns. "She's scary!"
The Black Widow Spider enters and unties a length of black silk that is attached to the top of the tent. She climbs up the black silk, turning upside down and swinging as she climbs.

Once at the top, she reaches over and tugs at a length of red silk that is also hanging from the top of the tent. It unfurls, and out of it, tumbling over and over, is the ringmaster, Gentleman George.

Everyone screams as he drops. Then he twists and grabs the silk, stopping just before hitting the floor. Everyone cheers. He lands on his feet and chases after the clowns, who run away as quickly as they can.

The circus performance has finished. Hanako and Ken are still giggling as they walk out of the big tent with Granny and Granddad. They see Sam at the exit and wave.
"Did you have fun at the show?" she says.
"We had a fantastic time!" says Ken.
"Yes!" adds Hanako. "The clowns tell jokes that are more terrible than our Granddad's!"